The Boyhood Diary of

Charles Lindbergh,

1913-1916:

Early Adventures of the Famous Aviator

Edited by Megan O'Hara

Content Consultant:
Donald H. Westfall, Historic Site Manager
Charles A. Lindbergh House State Historic Site,
Little Falls, Minnesota

Blue Earth Books

an imprint of Capstone Press
Mankato, Minnesota

Blue Earth Books are published by Capstone Press
151 Good Counsel Drive, P.O. Box 669, Mankato, Minnesota 56002
http://www.capstone-press.com

Library of Congress Cataloging-in-Publication Data
Lindbergh, Charles
    Charles A. Lindbergh, Jr. : the boyhood diary of Charles Lindbergh, 1913–1916:
    early adventures of the famous aviator / edited by Megan O'Hara.
    p. cm. – (Diaries, letters and memoirs)
    Includes bibliographical references (p. 31) and index.
    ISBN 0-7368-0600-8
    1. Lindbergh, Charles A. (Charles Augustus), 1902–1974— Diaries—Juvenile literature.
2. Lindbergh, Charles A. (Charles Augustus),1902–1974—Childhood and youth—Juvenile
literature. 3. Air pilots—United States—Diaries—Juvenile literature. [1. Lindbergh, Charles
A. (Charles Augustus), 1902–1974—Childhood and youth. 2. Airpilots. 3. Diaries.] I. Title.
II. Series.
    TL540.L5 A4 2001
    629.13'092—dc21
    [B]   00-036766

Summary: Excerpts from the boyhood diary of Charles Lindbergh, including
entries detailing passenger train travel, camping along the Mississippi River, and
an automobile trip around rural Minnesota. Supplemented by sidebars, activities,
and a timeline of the era.

Editorial credits
Editor: Kay M. Olson
Designer: Heather Kindseth
Illustrator: Linda Clavel
Photo researchers: Heidi Schoof and
    Kimberly Danger
Artistic effects: Louise Sturm-McLaughlin

Photo credits
Minnesota Historical Society, cover, cover
background, 5, 6, 7, 11, 15, 17, 18, 19, 20,
21, 23, 26, 27, 28 (bottom), 29 (bottom);
Library of Congress, 8, 9; Minnesota
Department of Natural Resources, 13;
Archive Photos, 28 (top), 29 (top, left);
FPG International, 29 (top, right)

1 2 3 4 5 6 06 05 04 03 02 01

CONTENTS

Editor's Note

The Diaries, Letters, and Memoirs series introduces real young people from different time periods in U.S. history. Whenever possible, the diary entries in this book appear word for word as they were written in the young person's original diary. Because the diary appears in its original form, you will notice some misspellings and mistakes in grammar. To clarify the writer's meaning, corrections or explanations within a set of brackets sometimes follow the misspellings and mistakes.

This book contains only portions of Charles Lindbergh's boyhood diary. Text sometimes has been removed from the individual diary entries. In these cases, you will notice three dots in a row, which are called ellipses. Ellipses show that words or sentences are missing.

A more complete version of Charles Lindbergh's boyhood diaries is currently held at the Minnesota Historical Society in St. Paul, Minnesota.

"When I was a child on our Minnesota farm, I spent hours lying on my back in high timothy and redtop, hidden from passersby, watching white cumulus clouds drift overhead, staring into the sky. It was a different world up there. You had to be flat on your back, screened by grass stalks, to live in it. How wonderful it would be, I'd thought, if I had an airplane—wings with which I could fly up to the clouds and explore their caves and canyons—wings like that hawk circling above me. Then, I would ride on the wind and be part of the sky . . . "

—*Charles Lindbergh*

Charles Lindbergh
The Boyhood Diary of the Famous Aviator

Charles Augustus Lindbergh Jr. was born on February 4, 1902, one year before the Wright Brothers made the world's first airplane flight. As an adult, Charles was the first person to fly an airplane across the Atlantic Ocean. He made a solo flight between New York and Paris, France. But before Charles Lindbergh became known as the "Lone Eagle," he was an adventurous and active boy. He spent the spring and summer living in Minnesota and the rest of the year living in Washington, D.C. Before he learned to fly, Charles Lindbergh was an independent young man who conducted experiments in his grandfather's laboratory, drove and repaired automobiles, and managed the family farm.

Charles' parents gave their son opportunities that few other children had at the time. From 1907 to 1917, Charles' father, Charles A. Lindbergh Sr., served as a Minnesota congressman in the U.S. House of Representatives. Charles' father often brought him to the U.S. Capitol, where Charles listened to political speeches.

As an 11-year-old, Charles learned to drive the family's Model T. In 1916, Charles drove his father on campaign stops throughout rural Minnesota. The country roads were muddy and deeply rutted, making driving a constant challenge. The automobile sometimes would sink up to its fenders in slippery mud. Other times the engine would stop suddenly. Charles tinkered with the car engine until it worked again.

Charles posed for this photo in 1905 when he was about 3 years old.

6

In the spring of 1916, Charles recorded the automobile trip he took with his father, who was campaigning for the U.S. Senate. Charles drove his father's car, a Saxon Six.

Each spring and summer, Charles and his mother, Evangeline, stayed at the family home in Little Falls, Minnesota. They called this summer home "camp." Charles spent his days in the fields and on the Mississippi River. He swam with friends in Pike Creek. He sometimes played in the empty upstairs rooms of the house. One day, Charles heard the sound of an unusual engine. He thought it was too loud and too fast to be an automobile. He climbed out the second-story window and onto the roof to see what was making the noise. Charles got his first glimpse of an airplane.

In Minnesota, Charles and his father went hunting, fishing, and camping. They watched deer, beaver, and other wildlife. Charles enjoyed fishing and sleeping in a tent under the stars. When he was a famous aviator, Charles would still pitch a tent under a wing of his airplane. There, in a quiet farm field, he could escape noisy crowds and catch a good night's rest.

From age 11 to age 14, Charles kept a diary. The diary entries tell about different times in his childhood. The first setting is on the train ride he and his mother took each fall from Minnesota to Washington, D.C. Another diary scene is a camping trip Charles and his father took, traveling from the headwaters of the Mississippi down part of the river. The final setting describes an automobile trip around Minnesota. Charles drove while his father campaigned for a seat in the U.S. Senate.

The Diary of Charles Lindbergh

*Each fall during his childhood, Charles and his mother
traveled by train from Little Falls, Minnesota, to Detroit,
Michigan. There they visited Grandfather and
Grandmother Land. Charles Land was a dentist and an
inventor. He had a laboratory in his basement and let
young Charles use many of his tools, machinery,
and chemicals. After Charles and his mother
stayed a few weeks in Detroit, they headed
for Washington, D.C., by train.*

. . . from Detroit [Michigan] to [Washington,] D.C.
Oct. 29. 1913—

I got on the train 15 minutes before it started . . . in no time it seemed that we
had gotten to Tolledo [Toledo, Ohio] which is 60 miles [96 kilometers] from
Detroit . . . we are passing the longest traffick bridge I ever saw . . . over some river
that I don't know the name of . . . we are going under lots of streetes and are
cutting through peoples back yards and back houses we are now in the part that
was fludded so last year that we couldnot come over this line . . . I like to go
through tunnels and around hills which we also go around in the night but one
thing I was glad of that was that we go through the baltimore tunnel in the
morning that is the longest of the tunels on this line . . . the train is tipping so it
almost looks as if it would fall over on its side mother is scard [scared] that it will
. . . we will arrive in Washington D.C. at eight am in the morning . . . the waiter is
going up to start the first call for supper after supper the porter will make up our
bearth [bed]. everybody is going to wash for supper . . .

Passenger Trains

In the early 1900s, trains were the easiest way for people to travel. At this time, more than 1,000 railroad companies and more than 37,000 steam locomotives operated in the United States.

A station bustled with excitement when a train whistled, announcing its arrival and warning people to clear the tracks. The train came into the station in a swirl of steam from the engine. A porter from each passenger car stepped out and put down a step for the passengers to enter or exit the train car. The porters loaded and unloaded passengers' luggage.

The conductor called out "All aboard!" when the train was ready to leave the station. The brakeman waved a red lantern to signal the engineer to start. The conductor and brakeman jumped aboard as the train gathered speed. Passengers sat in seats along narrow aisles, in small private compartments, or in larger areas called drawing rooms. Reaching a destination by train often took several days. The passenger cars had washrooms and sleeping areas called berths. First-class compartments had a drawing room or sitting room.

In 1865, George Pullman introduced sleeping cars on his trains. Soon after, Pullman added first-class dining cars. Dining cars had white starched linen tablecloths and elegant silverware on the tables.

The U.S Congress

The lawmaking body of the United States is the U.S. Congress. The U.S. Congress is made up of the Senate and the House of Representatives. The Senate has 100 members, two from each state. Senators serve a term of six years. The House of Representatives has 435 members. Each state's number of representatives depends on its population. States with more people have more representatives than states with fewer people. House members are elected to serve two-year terms.

The U.S. Constitution has given many powers to Congress. The chief power is to make laws for the United States. Congress also has the power to govern trade, collect taxes, coin money, establish post offices, and declare war.

Both houses of Congress have special duties and powers. The Senate has the power to approve or disapprove of the people the president appoints to certain positions. The House of Representatives has the duty of beginning all new laws about taxes and other money earned by the government.

Mar 4, '15—

The Last Day of Congres [Congress] I stayed out of school to see the closeing day. as I went into the house lobby about 9 a m Father asked a door-keeper what he thought about it The house was supposed to cloose [close] at 12 noon and yet that dumb doorkeeper said an extra session was to be called. The house was attending to ordinary matters and no booring speeches were made until about 11 am when Underwood got up and lauded the speeker . . . a bill was put up 5 mins or 10 before 12 . . . after 15 mins was up the speaker got up and said "the hour of 12 having arived the house is adjourned["] . . .

During the summer and fall of 1915, Charles and his father made a two-part expedition down a section of the Mississippi River. They began their journey by taking a train to the town of Bemidji in north central Minnesota. From there, they towed their boat to Lake Itasca, the headwaters of the Mississippi River. They traveled by boat through forests, swamps, and rapids. Toward the end of June, Charles and his father stored their boat at Cass Lake and returned to Little Falls by train. Later that fall, they retrieved their boat and continued the river journey.

June 18 – [19]15—

. . . Itasca is not as wide as the Mississippi is where camp [home] is there we took the boat down to the dock and went back to eat supper after which we went down to where the beever [beaver] build[s] a dam every night and the proprieter tears it down every day . . . I chopped down a few beaver stumps and we walked around the lake a little way where we looked back and saw a deer it threw up its tail and ran up the hill . . . there were lots of deer tracks on the road some doe and some buck later we took a search light and went down to see if we couldnt see some of the beaver at work after waiting about 15 mins

Charles liked sleeping outdoors, whether he was camping or at home. He made the family's screened-in porch his bedroom and spent all but the coldest nights sleeping there.

11

we had a falce alarm as a head came towards us but it was only a muscrat in about an hour we saw a head of a beaver . . . we could see the water where it jumped in . . . it came nearer and finally stop[p]ed a few feet away to look around we could see it pretty well then it came right in front of us and I turned on the light it threw a few rays on father, the beaver looked up and seeing him swam away with a splash of its tail . . . we could hear them drag[g]ing the trees for the dam and after that we went away

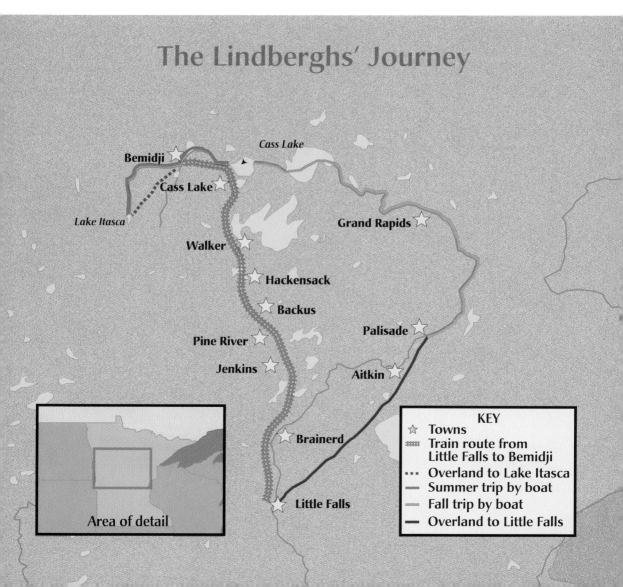

The Lindberghs' Journey

KEY
☆ Towns
▥ Train route from Little Falls to Bemidji
··· Overland to Lake Itasca
— Summer trip by boat
— Fall trip by boat
— Overland to Little Falls

Area of detail

Itasca State Park

The Mississippi River begins as a small stream flowing out of Lake Itasca in north central Minnesota. In 1891, the Minnesota legislature passed a bill making Itasca the state's first state park. This legislation preserved the wilderness area of trees, lakes, and historic headwaters of the Mississippi River.

Itasca is one of Minnesota's most visited state parks. At the headwaters area, visitors can walk on stepping stones across the little stream that feeds the Mississippi River. This state park is made up of more than 32,000 acres (1,300 hectares) of land and more than 100 lakes formed from glaciers more than 20,000 years ago.

Tracking Wildlife

Charles enjoyed looking for animal tracks. You can learn about animals by studying the size of their tracks and the distance between each track.

What You Need:

measuring stick about
  3 feet (1 meter) long
small rubber bands

pocket mirror or flashlight
notebook and pencil
books about animal tracks

What you do:

1. Look for tracks in mud, wet sand, or soft dirt. Nature trails, riverbanks, beaches, and fresh snow are good places to look for animal tracks.
2. Position yourself so that the animal track is between you and the sun. Shadows in the track will make it stand out more clearly. Use a flashlight or a pocket mirror to reflect light into a track to highlight its details.
3. Measure the length of the animal track with the measuring stick. Wrap a rubber band around the measuring stick to mark the measurement.
4. Make a sketch of the track to help you identify it later. Lay the portion of the measuring stick marking the track length on a page in your notebook. With a pencil, mark the top and bottom of the track length. Next sketch the shape of the track within the pencil marks.
5. Measure the animal's stride. Wrap a second rubber band around the measuring stick to mark the distance from the heel of one animal track to the heel of its next track.
6. Hold the measuring stick at the stride measurement mark. Hold this portion of the measuring stick above the heel of the second track. Sweep the point of the measuring stick in an arc and look for the next track in the trail.
7. Keep a record in your notebook of the types of animal tracks you find. Include information such as when and where you found the tracks.
8. Look in your library for books on animal tracks. Use the illustrations and photographs to identify the tracks you have sketched.

June 19, '15—

. . . we went to breakfast and then started out to Elk Lake . . . after passing about three lakes we came to Elk Lake   some people say that it is the source of the Mississippi I do to[o] because there is a little brook that flows from it to Itasca . . .

After their noon meal, Charles and his father practiced pitching the tent. They packed the boat and started on their river journey.

. . . I took the oars first and Father the paddle after we thought we saw where the lake branched three times and they only turned out to be bays we came to the big fork where the Forest rese[a]rch has a station we reached the Miss[issippi] river it is only about 20 feet [6 meters] wide there are hundreds of turtles and fish in about a mile [1.6 kilometers] we came to a dam where we decided to camp for the night

As an adult, Charles remembered his happy summer days in a letter to his mother. He wrote, "I am not happy living away from water . . . "

June 20—

. . . we went through miles of swamp where the river was affully [awfully] crooked it started raining . . . after we got a few miles it stopped raining and we saw some baby ducks down the river . . . it started raining again and to make it worse we came to a dam that was broken we had to unload all the stuff and lower the boat down with roots it was raining all the time . . .

June 21—

. . . I have not had shoes on for two days . . . we found a nice place to pitch the tent it was on a bluff among the jack pines . . . I shot a couple of times at some flocks of blackbirds . . . then we went to bed I am writing now in the tent it is so dark that I can hardly see to write but it feels comfortable so far anyway

June 22—

. . . father couldn't sleep at all he said that there were to[o] many mosquitos around . . . we got up and started breakfast . . . we finally got away into the boat . . . it was about 3 oclock and father was bound to get to a house for the night saying he couldn't sleep in a tent with mosquitos . . . at 7 oclock we came in sight of a house . . . the people said that it was 7 miles [11 kilometers] to Bemidji Father asked them how far by river and they said it was shorter we found out afterwards that it was 25 miles [40 kilometers] . . . we finished supper and went to bed after having made the record run of 60 miles [97 kilometers] that day

June 23—

We got up today at 15 to 6 ate and started . . . we came to a willow country together with the ordinary trees populars [poplars] a few pines and hard wood the river is overflowing the banks here . . . I had to use the oars pretty hard to get out in the middle of the river the river is about 100 feet [30 meters] wide as an average it is very high when we came near Rice Lake and joined the Little Mississippi yesterday it was overflowing and nearly threw as much water into the Mississippi as was there . . .

When Charles was a baby, his mother kept him outside as much as possible, even during winter. Charles grew up loving the outdoors.

By the time the Lindberghs reached Lake Bemidji, Charles noted that they had passed 17 creeks and seven rivers. After stopping to fish, Charles and his father spent the night in a hotel in the town of Bemidji.

June 24—

> We leave here for Cass Lake this morning . . . on our way down a little launch was going to go over to the mouth of the river just where we wanted to go so father asked . . . if we could get a tow . . . in about 2½ hrs we had made the trip from the lake to the dam . . . there were 2 men sitting fishing about 50 feet [15 meters] away they said they would help us make the portage so father went around to find out if he would get some dinner I said it would be more fun to eat in the boat but he said there was no use roughing it when we didnt have to . . .

Charles and his father went hunting during the second half of their trip down the Mississippi River. The father and son had a rule to never shoot at a bird unless it was in flight.

When Charles and his father reached Cass Lake, they stored their boat and went to Bemidji to take the train back to Little Falls. They planned to finish the trip in the fall, when they could also do some hunting. In April of 1916, Charles finished recording what happened on the second part of the journey.

[Fall 1915]—

    During the summer there was some uncertainty about me going the rest of the trip but at the last minute I went . . . I dont remember just how we got to Cass Lake but we did . . . I had my automatic and father the double barrel shotgun besides the extra hunting equipment . . . Somewhere down the river we met the government launch which gave us a tow to the barges where the channel was being dug . . . the next day they gave us a tow to a place just above Grand Rapids . . . At G.R. I got a new camera as my old one got wet when we were being towed by the launce [launch] it cost $6. We also bought a $90 motor which after a great deal of trouble installed and after much more trouble made to go and we started off with a two days delay. The motor was awful it would start go an hour and stop and it took another hour to get it going again . . .

When after long delays on account of the Koban which is the name of the motor we reached Palisade . . . the next day the motor would not go at all and after half a days labor we hired a toe [tow] for $12 to akin [Aitkin] 70 miles [110 kilometers] away . . . when we were getting into Aitken the row boat got loose and we had to go back for it. From Aitken we shipped to Little Falls where we were already overdue.

Charles and his mother gave their house in Little Falls, Minnesota, the name "camp." Later in his life, Charles wrote about the outdoor fun he had during his summers there.

Early Automobiles

In the early 1900s, more than 400 automobile companies were making horseless carriages. The most successful of these early car makers was Henry Ford. His Model T forever changed the automobile industry, as well as the way people traveled. On October 1, 1908, Ford sold the first Model T for $825. More than 15 million Model Ts were sold between 1908 and 1927.

Early automobiles were much different than the cars of today. Instead of turning a key, the driver had to turn a crank to start the engine. Whenever the engine stalled, the driver had to get out of the car, walk to the front, insert the lever, and crank the engine until it started. Many car models had no roof, or had a folding top made out of canvas or other heavy fabric. Cars ran on thin tires with rubber innertubes, which often got holes and went flat.

Safety and comfort features were not found on early model cars. There were no seat belts, no heaters, and sometimes there were no windshields. Service stations offered gasoline for sale, but they seldom had parts or tools to repair stalled cars. Drivers had to carry along tools, spare tires, innertube patches, and tire pumps wherever they went.

Charles drove his father around Minnesota in a Saxon Six automobile during the 1916 campaign for the U.S. Senate.

20

*Charles Lindbergh Sr.
was a lawyer and a U.S.
Congressman. His father
was born in Sweden and had
been active in politics there.*

*Charles Lindbergh Sr. was a
member of the U.S. House of
Representatives. In 1916, he
began a campaign for election to
the U.S. Senate. He invited
14-year-old Charles to drive the
car on the campaign around the state of Minnesota. Charles was in charge of driving
the Saxon Six automobile, making mechanical repairs, and reading maps.*

Auto Trip Spring 1916
April 22 [19]16—

>We started from Washington [D.C.] . . . and took a train to Chicago and intend to go from there to Minneapolis and from there to Melrose [in Minnesota] where the campaign will be opened. In Minneapolis I will learn to run a Saxon Six [automobile] . . .

Monday Apr 24 2⁴⁵ PM—

>We got into Minneapolis at 7⁵⁰ A M . . . we walked to the saxon place . . . We purchased some supplies as outer tire extra etc and then the man . . . took me to a side street and taught me to run the car. The Saxon he said was the best car he ever rode in. I am now waiting for Father at the hotel he is already 15 min. late.

April Tuesday 25 10 PM—

. . . We got the car out at two and after going around the city two hours we
started for St Cloud The rodes [roads] are fine We averaged about 25
miles [40 kilometers] per hour all the way. We got 5 gallons [19 liters] of
gasoline at Deer river and when we got to Clear lake the needle
registered none but as we couldnt get any there we went on to St
Cloud and the gass lasted all the way . . .

April 26—

I got up at 6 this morning Father went to Melrose by train as the
roads are very bad I took the car to the Saxon Agency here and they
replaced a valve which was leaking gas from one of their own cars
for 75¢ . . .

May 1 1916 9⁴⁵ PM—

. . . It was snowing badly outside, and we had to make the trip to
Minneapolis with curtains on but they kept us warm as it was so
very cold outside . . .

May 5 10 PM—

We left Minneapolis at two and went to Anoka where Father saw a man.
From there we went to Deer River where we saw a few people and had
supper. Then we started for Cambridge and it was soon dark. We got off
the road several times but finally got to St Francis and as the road was
straight and fairly good we went to Isanti for the night.

May 7—

When I got to the car I found it short circuted on account of
the horn. I had to crank it and take it to the Saxon place
where for $2.00 I got a new horn . . .

May 10, 10 PM—

. . . The wind is the worst to-day than it has been before . . . It takes lots
more gasoline and oil. Some of the roads are awful. We almost got stuck some places.
Today I pumped the tires for the first time. They have gown [gone] 1000 miles
[1,600 kilometers] without pumping We went 130 miles [210 kilometers] to-day . . .

22

Charles grew up surrounded by animals. With few children nearby, dogs often were the only playmates Charles had. Here he poses with his pet, Dingo.

May 15—

It rained all today and we got the auto filled with speeches and suitcases but couldnt start [for Duluth]. We went around the city some and when the car was going down a hill I had to put on breaks [brakes] to stop before the open door of a street car the car skidded and I couldnt stop it The people getting on the [street]car ran for posts lamps and telephone [poles] or anything handy and the car went every which way but finally I got it under control again . . .

May 18—

. . . When we were about 16 miles [26 kilometers] from Duluth the gas got low and we didnt know if we had enough to last us or not and there were no side stations before West Duluth so when we got to the top of one of the many hills which surround Duluth we would turn off the gas and let the machine coast down. This went all right until we got to the top of the highest hill looking over West Duluth and we started to coast down but the hill got steeper and steeper and as it curved around a lot we could not see the end of it. Then I put on breaks [brakes] that stopped the progress until they got loose and the hill got steeper We were going so fast that the gear wouldnt go in and then in front of us down the steepest part of the hill was the railroad track and a freighter in the middle. The gate was down and there was no way to stop . . . There was a slight opening (about the width of the car[)] between the gate and the track and full of deep clay. I turned into that and as there was nothing could go through it we stopped in about ten feet [3 meters] nothing was hurt but there was no getting out of that hole . . . Then the yardmaster came along and offered us a tow out with a locomotive that was near by. When it got on the cable it just lifted the car right out and we went on . . .

May 21, 1916—

To-day we went out to the brass works . . . In the evening we went to the steel works and gave out a lot of speeches.

May 26—

To-day I went to St Paul and around this city a little. We are averaging 300 miles [480 kilometers] in four days . . .

June 4—

We started this afternoon about four and went to Hastings . . . From Hastings we went to Red Wing and from there to Lake City by night We could not see much on account of the dark but it is said to be one of the most beautiful places in the state. the country is getting very hilly.

June 8—

We went to St Paul this evening and worked minneapolis this morning.

Starting Your Own Diary

Charles recorded special activities and events in his boyhood diary. He wrote about camping with his father and about taking a train trip with his mother. He wrote about driving through the country roads of Minnesota. All of these subjects are great topics for a journal. You can keep a journal to record your life and what happens in the world each day. People sometimes keep diaries all their lives. Diaries can become personal histories. Someday your diary might be a book like Charles'.

What You Need
Paper: Use a blank book, a diary with a lock, or a notebook. Choose your favorite.
Pen: Choose a special pen or use different pens. You might want to use different colors to match your different moods.
Private time: Some people write before they fall asleep. Others write when they wake up. Be sure you have time to put down your thoughts without interruptions.

What You Do
1. Begin each entry in your diary with the day and date. This step helps you remember when things happened. You can go back and read about what you did a week ago, a month ago, or a year ago.
2. Write about anything that interests you. Write about what you did today. Describe people you saw, what you studied, and songs you heard.
3. Talk about your feelings. Describe what makes you happy or sad. Give your opinions about things you see, hear, or read.
4. Write in your diary regularly.

When he was a boy, Charles' mother told him that flying was dangerous and expensive. As a young man, Charles became the world's most famous pilot.

Afterword

Although Congressman Lindbergh spoke out against U.S. involvement in World War I (1914-1918), the United States entered the war in April 1917. That winter, Charles left school during his senior year. He received full academic credit because he was willing to farm at the family's Minnesota home. Farm workers were badly needed to replace the men drafted for military service.

In 1920, Charles studied mechanical engineering at the University of Wisconsin. He left college to learn to fly. In 1925, he became chief pilot for an airmail service, flying in all weather conditions.

Raymond Orteig challenged pilots around the world in 1919. This New York businessman offered $25,000 to the first pilot who could fly an airplane nonstop between New York and Paris, France. Some pilots had tried the feat but no one had been successful. Charles was one of many young pilots who were eager to try.

On May 20, 1927, Charles Lindbergh took off from New York in a plane he designed himself. The businessmen who helped Charles pay to have the plane built named it the *Spirit of St. Louis*. Charles flew solo across the Atlantic Ocean and landed safely in France more than 33 hours after leaving New York. People gave him the nickname "Lone Eagle" because he had completed the heroic feat alone.

Charles became a celebrity all over the world as soon as he landed. A crowd of about 150,000 people greeted him at the airfield in France. On June 11, 1927, President Calvin Coolidge presented Charles with the Distinguished Flying Cross. Two days later, 4 million people came to see Charles in a New York parade. The cheers and attention followed Charles wherever he went.

On May 27, 1929, Charles married Anne Morrow. Charles taught Anne to fly airplanes. She was the navigator and radio operator for their many flights around the world. Together, they surveyed routes for air travel.

In 1932, Charles and Anne moved to Hopewell, New Jersey, with 18-month-old Charles Jr. The Lindberghs wanted to protect their son from the fans, photographers, and reporters who followed the Lindberghs wherever they went. But Charles Jr. was kidnapped one month after the family moved to Hopewell. Ten weeks after the baby had been taken from his crib, searchers found him dead near the Lindbergh home. A jury found Bruno Hauptmann guilty of the child's kidnapping and murder. After the trial, Charles and Anne moved to England.

In 1939, the Lindberghs moved back to the United States. Charles spoke out against U.S. involvement in World War II (1939-1945). But when the United States entered the war in 1941, Charles helped his country by test-flying new airplanes and flying combat missions.

Charles worked hard at activities that interested him. He was an environmentalist and worked with the World Wildlife Fund to protect whales from extinction. Charles helped develop a perfusion pump, a forerunner of today's heart-lung machine. He worked in early rocket research and in worldwide commercial aviation.

In 1972, doctors diagnosed Charles with cancer. He died on August 26, 1974, and was buried near his home on Maui, Hawaii.

People called Charles the Lone Eagle after his solo flight across the Atlantic.

Timeline

The Wright Brothers make the first airplane flight at Kitty Hawk, North Carolina.

Raymond Orteig offers $25,000 to the first pilot to fly nonstop between New York and Paris.

1902   1903   1917   1919   1927

February 4– Charles Lindbergh is born in Detroit.

Charles leaves high school to tend the family's farm.

Charles makes the first solo flight across the Atlantic Ocean from New York to Paris, France.

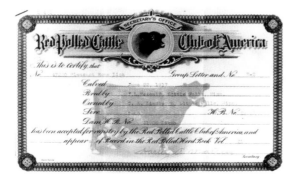

The United
States enters
World War II.

American astronauts land on the moon.

1941   **1953**   **1969**   **1974**

Charles' book
*The Spirit of
St. Louis*, is
published.

Charles dies
of cancer on
August 26.

Words to Know

academic credit (ak-uh-DEH-mik KRED-it)—a school requirement that counts toward graduation

aviation (ay-vee-AY-shuhn)—the science of building and flying aircraft

berth (BURTH)—a bed in a train

cumulus (KYU-muh-luss)—flat-base cloud formations piled high and fluffy

environmentalist (en-VYE-ruhn-men-tal-uhst)—one who is concerned about the natural world of the land, sea, and air

headwaters (HED-waw-turs)—the source of a stream or river

laud (LAHWD)—to praise

mechanical engineering (muh-KAN-uh-kuhl en-juh-NEER-eng)—a branch of study concerned with mechanics and the production of tools and machinery

navigator (NAV-uh-gate-uhr)—one who uses maps, compasses, or the stars as a guide during travel

perfusion pump (puhr-FYOO-zhun PUHMP)—a type of machine that forces water through pipes

portage (POR-tij)—carrying a boat over land from one body of water to another

redtop (RED-top)—a type of lawn grass also grown for animal grazing

sluice (SLOOS)—an artificial passage for water

survey (SUR-vay)—to measure an area in order to make a map or plan

timothy (TIH-muh-thee)—a European grass grown for hay

Internet Sites

Charles Lindbergh
http://www.norfacad.pvt.k12.va.us/project/
lindbergh/lindbergh.htm

Charles A. Lindbergh Jr. Story
http://homeschooling.about.com/education/
homeschooling/library/bllindbergh.htm

**Charles A. and Anne Morrow
  Lindbergh Foundation**
http://www.lindberghfoundation.org

**World Book Encyclopedia: Two Legends
  of Aviation**
http://www.worldbook.com/fun/aviator/html/
twolegnd.htm

Places to Write and Visit

Charles A. and Anne Morrow
  Lindbergh Foundation
2150 Third Avenue North
Suite 310
Anoka, MN 55303-2200

Charles A. Lindbergh House State
  Historic Site
1620 Lindbergh Drive South
Little Falls, MN 56345

National Air and Space Museum
7th and Independence Avenue SW
Washington, DC 20560

National Aviation Museum
11 Aviation Parkway
Ottawa, Ontario
K1K 4R3
Canada

To Learn More

Davis, Lucile. *Charles Lindbergh.* Photo-Illustrated Biographies. Mankato, Minn.:
Bridgestone Books, 1999.

Giblin, James Cross. *Charles A. Lindbergh: A Human Hero.* New York: Clarion
Books, 1997.

Kent, Zachary. *Charles Lindbergh and the Spirit of St. Louis in American History.*
Berkley Heights, NJ: Enslow, 2001.

Lindbergh, Charles A. *Boyhood on the Upper Mississippi: A Reminiscent Letter.* St. Paul:
Minnesota Historical Society, 1972.

INDEX